LAUGH -Out- LOUD ULTIMATE JOKES for KIDS

2-IN-1 COLLECTION OF AWESOME JOKES AND ROAD TRIP JOKES

ROB ELLIOTT

HARPER

An Imprint of HarperCollinsPublishers

ISBN 978-0-06-256977-6

Typography by Gearbox

17 18 19 20 21   PC/LSCH   10 9 8 7 6 5 4 3 2 1

❖

First Edition

Laugh-Out-Loud
Awesome
Jokes for Kids

To my wife, Joanna. Everyone needs someone who helps them through the good days and bad—she's my awesome!

Q: Why can't you trust artists?

A: They're sketchy.

Q: Why did the baseball coach go to the bakery?

A: He needed a batter.

Q: What is a tree's favorite drink?

A: Root beer.

Q: Where do you take a bad rainbow?

A: To prism.

**Q: What kind of monster never irons
its clothes?**

A: A wash-and-wear-wolf.

Q: What do you call someone who grabs your cat and runs?

A: A purr snatcher.

Q: How do you get a bargain on a cruise vacation?

A: Look for a clearance sail.

Knock, knock.

Who's there?

To.

To who?

Don't you mean "to whom"?

Q: What did the buck say to the doe?

A: "I'm fawned of you, my deer."

Knock, knock.

Who's there?

Ache.

Ache who?

Bless you!

Bob: Did you hear about the farmer who wrote a joke book?

Bill: No, is it any good?

Bob: The jokes are pretty corny!

Knock, knock.

Who's there?

Hector.

Hector who?

When the Hector you going to open the door?

Emma: Can February March?

Leah: No, but April May!

Q: What do you call a nose with no body?

A: Nobody knows!

Q: Which has more courage, a rock or a tree?

A: A rock, because it's boulder!

Josh: Do you think change is hard?

Joe: I sure do! Have you ever tried to bend

a quarter?

Dave: Did you like my joke about the fish?

Adam: Not really.

Dave: Well, if you can think of a better fish joke, let minnow!

Isaiah: How smart are you, Mason?

Mason: I'm so bright my mom calls me "sun"!

Stanley: What happened when you found out your toaster wasn't waterproof?

Dudley: I was shocked!

Q: Why did the banana put on sunscreen?

A: It was starting to peel.

Q: Why did the Starburst go to school?

A: He wanted to be a Smartie!

Patient: Doctor, I think I'm turning into a piano.

Doctor: Well, that's just grand!

Q: Where do you learn to saw wood?

A: In a boarding school.

Q: What is a soda's favorite subject in school?

A: Fizz-ics!

Q: Why don't grapes snore when they're sleeping?

A: They don't want to wake the rest of the bunch.

Q: What's a cow's favorite painting?

A: The *Moo-na Lisa*.

Knock, knock.

Who's there?

Rita.

Rita who?

Rita good book lately?

Knock, knock.

Who's there?

Ears.

Ears who?

Ears looking at you, kid!

Q: What is a dentist's favorite time of day?

A: Tooth-thirty.

Q: What happens to toilet paper with good grades?

A: It goes on the honor roll!

Q: Which tree is always at the doctor's office?

A: A sick-amore tree!

Q: Why did the boy eat his homework?

A: Because the teacher said it was a piece of cake.

Q: What do you get when you throw noodles in a Jacuzzi?

A: Spaghetti.

Q: Why did the hog have a stomachache?

A: He pigged out at dinner.

Q: Why did the stereo blow up?

A: It was radioactive!

Q: How do you know when a bucket feels sick?

A: It looks a little pail.

Q: What plays music in your hair?

A: A headband!

Q: What kind of bird is with you at every meal?

A: A swallow.

Q: What goes ho-ho-ho, scratch-

scratch-scratch?

A: Santa Claws!

Q: What are a hyena's favorite cookies?

A: Snickerdoodles!

Q: Why couldn't the beaver work on

his computer?

A: He forgot to log in.

Q: What do you call a dog wearing earplugs?

A: It doesn't matter—it can't hear you anyway!

Q: How much did Santa's sleigh cost?

A: Nothing, it was on the house!

Q: What is a skeleton's favorite instrument?

A: A trombone.

Jenny: I should give my pig a bubble bath.

Johnny: That's hogwash!

Q: Why did the clock go back four seconds?

A: It was really hungry!

Q: Why did the clam go to the gym?

A: To work out its mussels.

Q: Why did the doctor send the book to the hospital?

A: It had to remove its appendix.

Jim: I need someone to help me build an ark.

Bob: I think I Noah guy!

Q: What do you call a fake noodle?

A: An im-pasta.

Q: What has four legs but can't walk?

A: A chair.

Q: What kind of shoes does a ninja wear?

A: Sneakers.

Q: Why don't frogs die from laryngitis?

A: Because they can't croak!

Q: Why was the eye doctor sent home from the party?

A: He was making a spectacle of himself.

Q: What kind of underwear does a lawyer wear?

A: Briefs.

Q: When does a hot dog get in trouble?

A: When it's being a brat.

Jimmy: That soda just hit me on the head!

Bobby: Oh no, are you OK?!

Jimmy: Yeah, luckily it was a soft drink.

Emma: Did you like your book about gravity?

Leah: Yes, I couldn't put it down!

Q: Why did the boy stop using his pencil?

A: It was pointless.

Q: Why did the ruler fail in school?

A: It didn't measure up.

Q: Why did the wood fall asleep?

A: It was board.

Q: Why did the bee need allergy medicine?

A: It had hives.

Q: What do you get when you cross a judge and a skunk?

A: Odor in the court!

Q: Why was the peanut mad at the pretzel?

A: It was in-salt-ing him.

Q: What kind of potato do you see on the news?

A: A commen-tater.

Q: Why did the pig get out of bed?

A: It was time to rise and swine!

Q: What is E. T. short for?

A: Because his legs are so little!

Q: What is the most negative month of the year?

A: November!

Q: How does a deer carry its lunch?

A: In a bucket!

Q: Why did the bee go to the barber?

A: He wanted a buzz cut.

Q: How do you make your shoe stay quiet?

A: Put a sock in it!

Q: What's a plumber's favorite instrument?

A: A pipe organ.

Q: Why shouldn't you have plastic surgery?

A: Because it's rude to pick your nose.

Q: Why did the baker have a rash?

A: Because he was making bread from scratch!

Q: How did the celery get rich?

A: It invested in the stalk market.

Q: What do you get when you throw a rooster in the bathroom?

A: A cock-a-doodle-loo!

Q: What do you call a can of Jell-O?

A: Gelatin.

Q: Who's in charge of the tissue company?

A: The handkerchief.

Q: How do owls like their rabbits for breakfast?

A: Bunny-side up!

Q: What do bunny rabbits eat in the summer?

A: Hop-sickles.

Q: Why do cannibals like dentists the best?

A: They're the most filling!

Q: **Why wouldn't the dentist tell the patient about his cavities?**

A: He didn't want to hurt his fillings!

Q: **Why did the egg get kicked out of the comedy club?**

A: He was telling bad yokes.

Q: **Why did Humpty Dumpty get sent to the principal's office?**

A: Because he was a rotten egg!

Q: **Why was the egg afraid to meet new people?**

A: He was a little chicken.

Q: What do you get when you wear a watch for a belt?

A: A waist of time!

Q: Why did the lumberjack chop down the wrong tree?

A: It was an axe-ident.

Q: Why did the chicken go to the gym?

A: It needed more eggs-ercise!

Q: Why did the rabbit go to the salon?

A: She was having a bad hare day.

Preston: Why did all the chickens disappear?

Winston: I don't have any eggs-planation!

Q: Who brings Easter eggs to all the

sea creatures?

A: The oyster bunny.

Q: What do you get when you cross a dog

and a crab?

A: A Doberman pincher.

Q: Why did the meteor do well in school?

A: It was the teacher's star pupil.

Q: What do you call a friendly scoop of frozen yogurt?

A: Nice cream!

Q: What do you call a mad biscuit?

A: A hot cross bun!

Q: Why did the baker study hard in school?

A: So he could make the honor roll!

Q: Why did the carpenter quit using his drill?

A: Because it was always boring.

Q: Why did the carpenter become a comedian?

A: He had a really funny drill bit.

Q: When doesn't a lamb spend any money?

A: When it's a sheep-skate!

Q: How does a blacksmith send a letter?

A: In an anvil-ope.

Q: What kind of room has no doors or windows?

A: A mushroom.

Q: **What kind of animal will fix your leaky pipes?**

A: A seal.

Q: **How many snails does it take to screw in a lightbulb?**

A: Who knows? Nobody waits around long enough to find out.

Q: **What kind of animals make the best detectives?**

A: Investigators!

Q: What does a soldier wear in the summer?

A: Tank tops.

Q: What kind of shoes make fun of you?

A: Mock-asins.

Q: What kind of clothes do houses wear?

A: Addresses.

Q: What did the conductor say to the

misbehaving violin?

A: "You're in treble!"

Jane: Where did you get your backpack?

Kate: That's a purse-onal question!

Q: What kind of dog uses a microscope?

A: A Labrador retriever.

Q: What do you call a sad cantaloupe?

A: Melon-choly.

Q: Where does a crocodile keep its milk?

A: In the refrige-gator.

Q: What do snowmen like on their cupcakes?

A: Frosting!

Q: Which kind of game makes you sneeze?

A: Domi-nose.

Q: When do sheepdogs cry?

A: When they're herding!

Q: What happened when the trees fell in love?

A: They got all sappy!

Bill: Did you like the sausage I cooked for you?

Joe: No, it was the wurst!

Q: How do you make a bug laugh?

A: Tickle it!

Q: **Why did the boy eat toaster waffles for breakfast, lunch, and dinner?**

A: His mom said he needed three square meals a day!

Q: **What do you call a camel with no humps?**

A: Humphrey.

Q: **What do you call a stick of dynamite that keeps coming back to you?**

A: A boomerang!

Q: **What did the stopwatch say to the clock?**

A: "Don't be alarmed!"

Q: Why did the fawn put on a sweater?

A: Because it was buck naked!

Q: What do you give to a sick horse?

A: Cough stirrup.

Q: Where does a sick sailor go?

A: To the dock-tor.

Q: What do you get when you cross a toad and a pig?

A: A warthog.

Q: Why did the pig want to be a comedian?

A: He was a big ham!

Q: What did the pirate say on his 80th birthday?

A: "Aye, matey!" (I'm 80)

Q: What do horses do when they fall in love?

A: They get mare-ied!

Q: How do you fix a squashed tomato?

A: With tomato paste.

Q: Why did the science teachers fall in love?

A: They had great chemistry.

Q: Why did the horse put her foal to bed?

A: It was pasture bedtime.

Ken: Do you like to eat venison?

Jen: It's deer-licious!

Q: Why do cows have hooves instead of feet?

A: Because they lactose. (lack toes)

Q: What do cows like to play at sleepovers?

A: Truth or Dairy.

Q: Why can't you trust a deer?

A: They'll always pass the buck.

Joe: You stole my cucumber!

Jon: What's the big dill?

Q: **What kind of exercise should you do after you eat fast food?**

A: Burpees.

Q: **How do pandas fight?**

A: With their bear hands.

Q: **What do you get when you cross a robot and a pirate?**

A: ARRRR2-D2.

Q: **What is a unicorn's favorite vegetable?**

A: Horn on the cob.

Q: What is a sheep's favorite fruit?

A: Baa-nanas.

Q: Why was the dentist mad at the schoolteacher?

A: She kept testing his patients.

Q: Where do fairies go to the bathroom?

A: In the glitter box.

Q: What do you get when you cross a fish and a camel?

A: A humpback whale.

Q: What do you get when you cross a skunk and an elephant?

A: A smelly-phant.

Q: How does a mouse open the door?

A: With a squeak-key.

Q: Where do you keep a skeleton?

A: In a rib cage.

Knock, knock.

Who's there?

Repeat.

Repeat who?

Who, who, who . . .

Q: How do you call an amoeba?

A: On a cell phone!

Q: How do you spot an ice-cream cone from far away?

A: With a tele-scoop.

Q: Why do you have to keep an eye on your art teacher at all times?

A: Because they're crafty.

Knock, knock.

Who's there?

Justin.

Justin who?

You're Justin time for dinner.

Knock, knock.

Who's there?

Howard.

Howard who?

Howard you like to let me inside?

Knock, knock.

Who's there?

Beets.

Beets who?

It beets me!

Q: What kind of fruit is never alone?

A: Pears.

Q: What does peanut butter wear to bed?

A: Jammies.

Knock, knock.

Who's there?

Cash.

Cash who?

No thanks, but do you have any almonds?

Knock, knock.

Who's there?

Feta.

Feta who?

I'm feta up with these knock-knock jokes!

Q: What did the frog wear with her dress?

A: Open-toad shoes.

Q: Where did the whales go on their date?

A: To a dive-in movie.

Knock, knock.

Who's there?

Lego.

Lego who?

Lego of the doorknob so I can come in!

Q: What happened when the rabbits got married?

A: They lived hoppily ever after.

Pete: Did you hear about the guy that invented knock-knock jokes?

Dave: No, what about him?

Pete: He just won the no-bell prize.

Q: Why did the banker quit his job?

A: He lost interest.

Knock, knock.

Who's there?

Minnow.

Minnow who?

Let minnow if you plan on letting me in!

Knock, knock.

Who's there?

Ada.

Ada who?

Ada lot of candy and now I feel sick.

Tim: Did you hear the joke about the roof?

Mark: No, what is it?

Tim: Never mind. It's over your head.

Q: What kind of nuts are always catching colds?

A: Cashews!

Knock, knock.

Who's there?

Espresso.

Espresso who?

Can I espresso much I want to come inside?

Q: What do you get when you cross an owl with
    a magician?

A: Who-dini!

Q: Why did the pony ask for a glass of water?

A: He was a little horse.

Q: What do you call it when candy canes decide
    to get married?

A: An engage-mint.

Q: What do you get if you scare a tree?

A: Petrified wood!

Q: How do you get straight A's?

A: Use a ruler.

Teacher: Please use a pencil for this test.

Student: What's the point?

Q: How did the music teacher open her classroom door?

A: She used a piano key.

Knock, knock.

Who's there?

Tibet.

Tibet who?

Early Tibet, early to rise.

Q: What do you get when you cross a rabbit and

a beetle?

A: Bugs Bunny.

Knock, knock.

Who's there?

Dishes.

Dishes who?

Dishes a funny knock-knock joke!

Q: What do sheep eat for breakfast?

A: Goat-meal.

Q: What happened when the banana married the orange?

A: They lived apple-y ever after.

Q: What do you call a girl who's always wrong?

A: Miss-informed.

Knock, knock.

Who's there?

Walnut.

Walnut who?

I walnut leave until you open the door!

Q: Why did the can stop talking to the can opener?

A: Because he kept trying to pry.

Q: What did one egg say to the other egg?

A: "All's shell that ends shell."

Q: What did the digital clock say to his mother?

A: "Look, Mom, no hands!"

Knock, knock.

Who's there?

Handsome.

Handsome who?

Handsome food to me—I'm starving!

Q: Why did the boy stop carving the stick?

A: He was a whittle tired.

Q: How does a farmer greet his cows?

A: With a milk shake.

Knock, knock.

Who's there?

Watson.

Watson who?

Watson the menu for dinner tonight?

Q: Why did the monsters run out of food at their party?

A: Because they all were a-goblin.

Q: What can you break without touching it?

A: A promise!

Q: What has to break before you can use it?

A: An egg!

Q: What do monkeys eat for lunch?

A: Gorilla cheese sandwiches.

Knock, knock.

Who's there?

Otter.

Otter who?

You otter let me in!

Anne: Are you sure you want another cat?

Jane: I'm paws-itive!

Q: Why did the music note drop out of college?

A: It couldn't pick a major.

Jim: I have a henway in my pocket!

Joe: What's a henway?

Jim: About four or five pounds.

Q: Why did the pig go into the kitchen?

A: It felt like bacon a cake.

Q: What do cats put in their iced tea?

A: Mice cubes.

Knock, knock.

Who's there?

Donut.

Donut who?

Donut make sense to let me in?

Q: What do you call a shape that isn't there?

A: An octo-gone.

Q: Why don't Dalmatians like hide-and-seek?

A: They're always spotted.

Knock, knock.

Who's there?

P.

P who?

I don't smell that bad!

Knock, knock.

Who's there?

Bean.

Bean who?

It's bean fun telling knock-knock jokes!

Q: What do you call an army of babies?

A: An infantry.

Q: Why couldn't the skunk go shopping?

A: He didn't have a cent. (scent)

Q: Why is it hard to have fish for dinner?

A: Because they're such picky eaters.

Knock, knock.

Who's there?

Romaine.

Romaine who?

Romaine calm and let me in!

Q: Why did the tuba stay after school?

A: Because it needed a tooter. (tutor)

Knock, knock.

Who's there?

Wheeze.

Wheeze who?

Wheeze going to tell a lot more knock-knock jokes!

Knock, knock.

Who's there?

Toad.

Toad who?

I toad you to let me in!

Knock, knock.

Who's there?

Pizza.

Pizza who?

You want a pizza me?!

Q: Where do pigs keep their dirty clothes?

A: In the hamper.

Q: What do you get if you're allergic to noodles?

A: Macaroni and sneeze.

Sue: I finally got my new alarm clock.

Sal: It's about time!

Q: What do golfers drink out of?

A: Tee-cups.

Q: What do dogs do when they're scared?

A: They flea! (flee)

Q: What did the baker say to the bread?

A: "I knead you!"

Q: What did the baker give his wife

   for Valentine's Day?

A: Candy and flours.

Q: What kind of bread has a bad attitude?

A: Sourdough.

Q: When is music sticky?

A: When it's on tape.

Hannah: Did you finish your panda costume

for Halloween?

Emily: Bearly!

Q: Where did the composer keep

his sheet music?

A: In a Bachs.

Q: What happened to the noodle that went down the drain?

A: He pasta way.

Q: What language do ducks speak?

A: Portu-geese.

Knock, knock.

Who's there?

Iguana.

Iguana who?

Iguana come inside and tell more jokes!

Q: Why did the chef quit making spaghetti sauce?

A: He ran out of thyme!

Q: What did the mommy elephant say to her baby?

A: "I love you a ton!"

Knock, knock.

Who's there?

Sid.

Sid who?

Sid down and I'll tell you some jokes!

Knock, knock.

Who's there?

Twister.

Twister who?

Twister key and unlock the door!

Q: Why was the cucumber so upset?

A: Because it was in a pickle.

Q: Why did the teacher take away the

kids' soda?

A: They failed their pop quiz.

Q: Why do monkeys like bananas?

A: They find them a-peeling.

Q: Where do cows go for lunch?

A: The calf-eteria.

Q: How do alligators give people a call?

A: They croco-dial the phone.

Q: How did the lizard remodel its bathroom?

A: With reptiles.

Knock, knock.

Who's there?

Moth.

Moth who?

Moth thumb got slammed in the door!

Knock, knock.

Who's there?

Aspen.

Aspen who?

Aspen wanting to tell more knock-knock jokes!

Tom: I don't want to finish my steak!

Mom: Quit beefing about it!

Knock, knock.

Who's there?

Annie.

Annie who?

Annie way you can open this door and let me in?

Q: Why did the baker go to the bank?

A: Because he kneaded more dough!

Joe: Do you like your new beard?

Phil: It's growing on me.

Q: How many animals did Moses take

on the ark?

A: None, it was Noah's ark!

Knock, knock.

Who's there?

Mustache.

Mustache who?

I mustache if you're going to let me in!

Q: What muscle never says "hello"?

A: A bye-cep!

Q: What kind of fruit is hard to chew?

A: A pome-granite!

Q: How does an angel light a candle?

A: With a match made in heaven.

Q: Where does spaghetti like to dance?

A: At the meatball.

Q: Why was the man running in circles around his bed?

A: He was trying to catch up on his sleep.

Q: What is a wasp's favorite hairstyle?

A: A beehive.

Q: What kind of bee likes sushi?

A: A wasa-bee. (wasabi)

Q: What kind of dessert do you eat in the bathtub?

A: Sponge cake.

Knock, knock.

Who's there?

Radio.

Radio who?

Radio not, here I come!

Knock, knock.

Who's there?

Turnip.

Turnip who?

Turnip the heat—it's freezing!

Q: Why did the panda join the choir?

A: He was a bear-itone!

Knock, knock.

Who's there?

Macon.

Macon who?

I'm Macon some eggs and bacon.

You want some?

Knock, knock.

Who's there?

Shell.

Shell who?

Shell be coming around the mountain when

she comes.

Q: When is butter contagious?

A: When it's spreading!

Knock, knock.

Who's there?

Hank.

Hank who?

Hank you for answering the door!

Knock, knock.

Who's there?

Mason.

Mason who?

It's pretty a-Mason that I'm still knocking after all these years!

Knock, knock.

Who's there?

Token.

Token who?

I'm token to you. Let me in!

Q: What kind of word can't wait to be used?

A: A now-n. (noun)

Q: Why did the skeleton's mom tell him to

eat more?

A: Because he was boney.

Q: What does Miss America drink?

A: Beau-tea!

Q: What do you call a locksmith that's in a bad mood?

A: Crank-key!

Knock, knock.

Who's there?

Izzy.

Izzy who?

Izzy going to open the door or not?

Knock, knock.

Who's there?

Butter.

Butter who?

You butter open up or else!

Knock, knock.

Who's there?

You.

You who?

I'm the one knocking, what do you want?!

Q: What do you call a really smart bug?

A: Brilli-ant!

Knock, knock.

Who's there?

Nose.

Nose who?

I nose you want to open the door, so go ahead.

Knock, knock.

Who's there?

Wool.

Wool who?

Wool you make me a sandwich?

Knock, knock.

Who's there?

Lena.

Lena who?

Lena little closer—I want to tell you a secret.

Q: **Why is the teacher in charge everywhere she goes?**

A: She controls all the rulers.

Q: **What do you call a cobra without clothes?**

A: S-naked.

Knock, knock.

Who's there?

Honeybee.

Honeybee who?

Honeybee a dear and open the door.

Knock, knock.

Who's there?

Peeka.

Peeka who?

No, it's peekaboo!

Knock, knock.

Who's there?

Colin.

Colin who?

Colin it a day! It's time to go.

Q: What is a chimpanzee's favorite drink?

A: Ape-le juice.

Q: Why couldn't the Little Pig run away from the Big Bad Wolf?

A: He pulled a hamstring!

Q: What is a bird's favorite subject in school?

A: Owl-gebra.

Q: Why was the bacon laughing so hard?

A: Because the egg cracked a yoke!

Knock, knock.

Who's there?

Waddle.

Waddle who?

Waddle I do if you don't open the door?

Knock, knock.

Who's there?

Hugo.

Hugo who?

**Hugo and tell mom I'm at
the door right now!**

Q: **Why does everybody like baby cows?**

A: They're adora-bull!

Knock, knock.

Who's there?

Gnat.

Gnat who?

It's gnat cool that I've been knocking all this time and you've still not opened the door!

Knock, knock.

Who's there?

Howl.

Howl who?

Howl I get in if you don't open the door?

Q: Why did the gorilla stop eating bananas?

A: He lost his ape-tite.

Q: Why was the oak tree so proud of his heritage?

A: Because his roots ran deep.

Knock, knock.

Who's there?

Honeycomb.

Honeycomb who?

Honeycomb your hair!

Q: What did the pig do when he wrote a book?

A: He used a pen name.

Q: What kind of flowers like to sing?

A: Pe-tune-ias.

Q: Why did the violin go to the gym?

A: So it could stay as fit as a fiddle.

Q: What does a baby ghost wear?

A: Bootees.

Joe: Can you believe my dog caught

a thousand sticks?

Jim: No, that sounds too far-fetched.

Q: How do you wash your stockings?

A: With a panty hose.

Q: Why did the vampire join the army?

A: So it could see combat!

Larry: I dreamed about a billboard.

Lucy: I think it's a sign!

Q: What do you get when paper towels fall asleep?

A: Napkins!

Q: What did the nurse say to the doctor?

A: "ICU!"

Q: How do you get your mom to make you some toast?

A: Just butter her up!

Knock, knock.

Who's there?

Casino.

Casino who?

Casino reason why you won't let me in.

Q: How do you buy a tropical fish?

A: With ane-money!

Q: Where should a wildcat sleep?

A: Behind a chain lynx fence!

Q: Why did the ape ask for lemons?

A: So it could be orangu-tangy!

Knock, knock.

Who's there?

Toucan.

Toucan who?

Toucan play at this game!

Knock, knock.

Who's there?

Alpaca.

Alpaca who?

Alpaca sandwich in my lunch box!

Q: How do you feel when a giant lizard steps on your toe?

A: Dino-sore!

Q: What's the funniest fish?

A: A piranha-ha-ha!

Q: What kind of bird lives in a mansion?

A: An ostrich!

Q: What was Beethoven's favorite vegetable?

A: Bach-choy!

Q: What do you get when you cross vegetables and animals?

A: Zoo-chini!

Q: What do you call a book with sparkles?

A: Glitter-ature!

Q: What do you call a bunch of cows that live together?

A: A com-MOO-nity.

Q: Where can you read about coffee cups?

A: In a mug-azine!

Q: Where can you read about insomnia?

A: In a snooze-paper.

Q: Who says bad words at the store?

A: A cuss-tomer.

Q: How do you pay for the truth?

A: With a reality check.

Q: How do you feel when your shirt is wrinkled?

A: Depressed!

Q: How does a whale pay for its lunch?

A: With curren-sea.

Q: How does the sun say hello?

A: With a heat wave!

Q: Why did the skunk have to stand in the corner?

A: It was a little stinker!

Valerie: Do you feel better about yesterday?

Malorie: Yes, I'm past tense!

Q: What do you call soap wearing a tuxedo?

A: A detergent!

Lou: What happened to all your furniture?

Sue: I gave it to chair-ity.

Ben: My pants almost fell down!

Ken: That was a clothes call!

Q: When is a nurse an artist?

A: When they're drawing blood.

Mary: How do you feel about your braces?

Molly: En-tooth-iastic!

Q: Why did the pirate share his secret treasure?

A: He wanted to get it off his chest.

Q: When must you open the door?

A: When you're obligated.

Q: Why did the diplomat become a brain surgeon?

A: He wanted peace of mind.

Q: How does a witch doctor stay in shape?

A: They hex-ercise!

Q: Why didn't the mice make cookies on Christmas Eve?

A: Because not a creature was stirring.

Knock, knock.

Who's there?

Design.

Design who?

Design says you're open, so let me in!

Q: How do you clean a pumpkin?

A: In a squashing machine.

Bella: You should write a book!

Stella: What a novel idea!

Q: What do you call it when you pass out the cards?

A: Ideal.

Q: What's the best time to get married?

A: On a Wednesday!

Q: What did one beekeeper say to the other?

A: "Mind your own buzz-iness!"

Q: What do you call a cow doing yoga?

A: Flexi-bull!

Q: What do bunnies like to play on

  the playground?

A: Hopscotch and jump rope!

Q: What do you call the selfie championships?

A: Olympics.

Q: Why did the boxer punch his oatmeal?

A: He was making his break-fist.

Q: Why did the meteorologist go home?

A: He was feeling under the weather.

Q: How is a professor like a thermometer?

A: They both have degrees.

Q: Why did the tooth fairy fall in love with the sandman?

A: She thought he was dreamy.

Q: What kind of bugs work at the bank?

A: Fine-ants.

Q: Where do you mail your clothes?

A: To your home address.

Q: Why don't dogs go to school?

A: They don't like arithme-tick.

Q: What's the funniest time of day?

A: The laughter-noon!

Q: What do you call a baby potato?

A: A tater tot!

Q: What do you call a zombie elephant?

A: Gro-tusk!

Q: What do you call a snowman that makes coffee?

A: A brrrr-ista.

Q: How does an artist cross the river?

A: He uses a drawbridge.

Q: What do beavers eat for breakfast?

A: Pas-trees.

Q: When is the storm coming?

A: Monsoon.

Q: What do you get when you cross a goldfish and a cupcake?

A: Muffins.

Q: Who takes care of a butterfly?

A: Its mother.

Knock, knock.

Who's there?

Jester.

Jester who?

Your jester one to open the door for me!

Knock, knock.

Who's there?

Hebrews.

Hebrews who?

Hebrews coffee every morning!

Knock, knock.

Who's there?

Howell.

Howell who?

Howell I get in if you don't open the door?

Q: What does a rabbit keep forever?

A: Its family hare-looms.

Diner: This soup is too bland!

Chef: That's in-salt-ing!

Q: Why did the little boy have so many vegetables?

A: He was a kinder-gardener!

Knock, knock.

Who's there?

Whitney.

Whitney who?

I can't Whitney longer for you to open this door!

Q: What happened when the anchorman broke his leg?

A: He got a newscast.

Q: What kind of bird wins the lottery?

A: A lucky duck!

Q: What do you get when everybody comes to the ball?

A: Perfect attendance.

Q: Why did the baker go to the square dance?

A: It wanted to dough-si-dough.

Q: When is a wig expensive?

A: When you have toupee.

Q: What do you call a beautiful zombie?

A: Drop-dead gorgeous.

Q: How does an artist get clean?

A: He draws a bath.

Q: How did the mop beat the broom in a race?

A: It left the broom in the dust.

Q: What happens if you get lost in the bathroom?

A: You don't know where to go.

Q: Who's in charge of the tooth fairy?

A: The presi-dentist.

Q: What does a wasp play at the park?

A: Frisbee!

Q: How do you feel after you steal all the blankets?

A: You have a quilt-y conscience.

Q: What do bees like on their cupcakes?

A: Frosting!

Jeff: We're getting a brand-new scale.

Steph: I can't weight!

Q: What's a spider's favorite book?

A: Webster's Dictionary.

Q: Why should you go in the woods when you're tired?

A: For rest!

Q: How do you say hello to an ice-cream cone?

A: "Fro-yo!"

Q: What's a bird's favorite cookie?

A: Chocolate chirp!

Q: What do you give a kitten to help it grow?

A: Fur-tilizer.

Knock, knock.

Who's there?

Mighty.

Mighty who?

Mighty want to open the door soon?

Knock, knock.

Who's there?

Wanda.

Wanda who?

Wanda come outside and play?

**Q: What do tornadoes use to keep
   their balance?**

A: Hurricanes.

Knock, knock.

Who's there?

Emma.

Emma who?

**Emma about to climb
   through the window!**

Knock, knock.

Who's there?

Isabella.

Isabella who?

**Isabella going to work or do I have to
keep knocking?**

Knock, knock.

Who's there?

Ava.

Ava who?

Ava got a good feeling about this.

Knock, knock.

Who's there?

Wyatt.

Wyatt who?

Wyatt taking you so long to answer the door?

Knock, knock.

Who's there?

Ruth.

Ruth who?

I have peanut butter stuck on the Ruth

   of my mouth!

Knock, knock.

Who's there?

Owen.

Owen who?

You're Owen a lot of money lately!

Q: What did the zombie wear to bed?

A: A night-goon.

Knock, knock.

Who's there?

Maya.

Maya who?

Maya help you with your coat?

Knock, knock.

Who's there?

Elise.

Elise who?

Elise I answer the door when people knock!

Q: What did the lemonade say to the iced tea?

A: "Hey, sweet tea." (sweetie)

Q: What do you call a lazy cow?

A: A meatloaf.

Knock, knock.

Who's there?

Quiche.

Quiche who?

Quiche me quick before I go!

Q: What kind of monster tucks you in at night?

A: A mom-bie.

Q: Why did the kids go to the haunted house?

A: It was eerie-sistible.

Miley: Do you want to go fishing with me?

Alex: That's a fin-tastic idea!

Q: What kind of money is easy to burn?

A: In-cents. (incense)

Knock, knock.

Who's there?

Yah.

Yah who?

What are you so excited about?

Knock, knock.

Who's there?

Lettuce.

Lettuce who?

Lettuce in and you'll find out!

Q: What's a pretzel's favorite game?

A: Twister.

Q: How do you make a milkshake?

A: Take it to a scary movie!

Knock, knock.

Who's there?

Luke.

Luke who?

Luke out the window and you will see.

Q: How did the banana get out of school?

A: It split!

Knock, knock.

Who's there?

Nana.

Nana who?

Nana your business!

Knock, knock.

Who's there?

Joanna.

Joanna who?

Joanna come out and play?

Knock, knock.

Who's there?

Ken.

Ken who?

Ken you tell me a funny knock-knock joke?

Knock, knock.

Who's there?

Ice cream soda.

Ice cream soda who?

Ice cream soda you can hear me!

Q: Why are babies good at math?

A: They have so much formula.

Q: How does the pirate put on his belt?

A: He swashbuckles it!

Q: Why was the nose sad?

A: Because everyone was picking on it.

Q: Why do fishermen have so many friends?

A: They're good at networking.

Q: What kind of bug is hard to understand?

A: A mumble-bee.

Q: Why did the school bus driver give the kids peanut butter sandwiches?

A: To go with the traffic jam.

Knock, knock.

Who's there?

Tomatoes.

Tomatoes who?

I'm freezing from my head tomatoes!

Q: Why did the dog go to the groomer?

A: It was looking a little ruff around the edges.

Knock, knock.

Who's there?

Granite.

Granite who?

Don't take me for granite!

Q: What do you call a fireman who runs away?

A: A smoke defector!

Q: Why did the snail drink a big cup of coffee?

A: It was feeling sluggish.

Q: Who gave the mermaid a new nose?

A: The plastic sturgeon.

Q: Why didn't the golfer get anything done?

A: He was just puttering around.

Q: What kind of dog does Santa have?

A: A Saint Brrrr-nard.

Q: What is Frankenstein's favorite book?

A: *The Scarlet Letter.*

Q: Why did the baker slice the bread?

A: He wanted to cut his carbs.

Q: What's a leprechaun's favorite kind

of music?

A: Shamrock!

Q: What happens when your pile of bills gets

too heavy?

A: You can't budget!

Q: What did the watch say to the clock?

A: "I don't want to wind up like you!"

Q: What do you get when you cross a flower and

a pickle?

A: A daffo-dill.

Q: When does a comedian tell the truth?

A: When he's a stand-up guy.

Q: What do you sing when you're in love?

A: A valen-tune!

Q: Why can't you win a fight with a dictionary?

A: It always has the last word.

Q: What's a boxer's favorite drink?

A: Punch!

Q: How does a chicken get over the flu?

A: It re-coop-erates.

Q: What do trees put on their salad?

A: Branch dressing.

Amy: Do you like your new hair color?

Ellie: Yes, I've dyed and gone to heaven!

George: I finally finished raking the yard.

James: That's a re-leaf!

Q: What's a plumber's favorite vegetable?

A: A leek!

Q: What happens if you check out too many library books?

A: You'll overdue it!

Q: Why did the farmer have a needle and thread?

A: He wanted to reap what he sewed.

Q: Why did Little Miss Muffet have a scale?

A: So she could have her curds and weigh.

Q: Why is the sun smarter than the moon?

A: The moon just isn't as bright.

Knock, knock.

Who's there?

Geyser.

Geyser who?

Geyser just as good at telling jokes as girls.

- -

Q: Who's in charge of the lumberjacks?

A: The board of directors.

Q: Where do you keep a baby pig?

A: In a playpen.

Q: When should you do your math homework?

A: Calcu-later.

Dad: Do you like how I ironed your shirt?

Mom: Yes, I'm impressed!

Q: When do you quit doing laundry?

A: When you throw in the towel.

Q: When doesn't a cannon work anymore?

A: When it gets fired!

Q: What do you get when you cross a trumpet and a watermelon?

A: A tootie fruity!

Q: What is an elephant's favorite dessert?

A: Hippopota-mousse.

Q: What's a farmer's favorite fairy tale?

A: "Beauty and the Beets."

Q: How do you carve a tombstone?

A: You engrave it.

Knock, knock.

Who's there?

Raymond.

Raymond who?

Raymond me to tell you another joke!

Q: What's a gorilla's favorite fruit?

A: Ape-ricots!

Q: How do you see a Dalmatian at night?

A: With a spotlight.

Knock, knock.

Who's there?

Window.

Window who?

Window I get to tell another joke?

Q: Why did the kids take the elevator?

A: Because it's not polite to stair.

Q: Why was the nose running?

A: So it wouldn't catch a cold.

Tongue twisters:

Green grass grows great.

Crushed nut clusters.

Ducks quack, chickens cluck.

My eyes spy pies.

Sheep sleep sweet.

Dump trucks drop rocks.

Q: What kind of animal eats lots of cheese?

A: The Hippopota-mouse.

Q: What is a grandma's favorite kind of cookie?

A: Gram crackers.

Sam: Did you like your karate class?

Marcus: I got a real kick out of it!

Q: Why was the mustard embarrassed?

A: It saw the salad dressing.

Q: What kind of cat likes to swim?

A: A platy-puss.

Q: When do boxers dress up in tuxedos?

A: When they want to look so-fist-icated.

Q: What happened when the stray dog was captured?

A: It gained a pound.

Knock, knock.

Who's there?

Juicy.

Juicy who?

Juicy any reason I shouldn't tell another knock-knock joke?

Knock, knock.

Who's there?

Alex.

Alex who?

Alex plain the joke later!

Q: What kind of birds always get stuck in trees?

A: Vel-crows.

Knock, knock.

Who's there?

Police.

Police who?

Police tell me this isn't the end of the

   knock-knock jokes!

Laugh-Out-Loud
Road Trip
Jokes for Kids

Joanna, Josh, Cassie, Emma, Leah, Anna, and Mason: I wouldn't want to travel through any adventure in life without you!

Q: Where do couples travel to get married?

A: To Marry-land! (Maryland)

Q: Where is the best place to go shopping

for clothes?

A: New Jersey.

Q: Which mountain has never been climbed?

A: Mount Never-est.

Q: Where's the best place to get a

kidney transplant?

A: Oregon. (organ)

Q: Where do people like to vacation over and over?

A: Michigan ... and igan and igan.

Q: What do you call a country with pink automobiles?

A: A car-nation.

Q: What is the cleanest state?

A: Wash-ington.

Knock, knock.

Who's there?

S'more.

S'more who?

Do you want to hear s'more road trip jokes?

Q: How did the zookeeper calm down the wild elephant?

A: With a trunk-quilizer.

Q: Why did Cinderella buy a camera?

A: So she could find her prints charming.

Knock, knock.

Who's there?

Zeke.

Zeke who?

Zeke and you will find!

Knock, knock.

Who's there?

Needle.

Needle who?

I needle little help getting this door open.

CAN YOU TAKE THE TRAIN
to the
LINCOLN MEMORIAL?

Tic - **TAC** - Toe

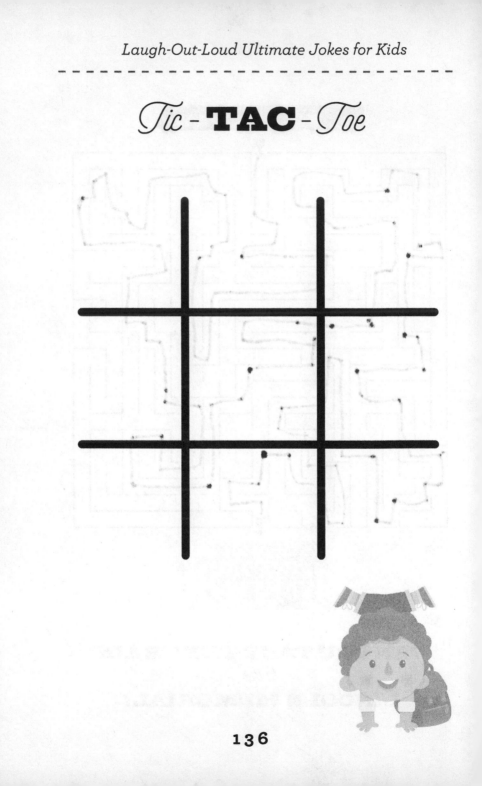

Q: Why did the man cry when he ran out of cola?

A: Because it was soda-pressing.

Knock, knock.

Who's there?

Launch.

Launch who?

Can we stop for launch yet?

Q: Why did the clock go on vacation?

A: It needed to unwind.

Knock, knock.

Who's there?

Anita.

Anita who?

Anita pull over and use the bathroom!

Q: What does a *Tyrannosaurus rex* eat while it's camping?

A: Dino-s'mores!

Knock, knock.

Who's there?

Spell.

Spell who?

W-h-o.

Q: What do you eat when you visit the Florida Everglades?

A: Marsh-mallows.

Q: What do sheep always take on a camping trip?

A: Their baa-ckpacks.

Q: Why can't you take a skunk on vacation?

A: Your trip will stink!

Q: Why should you always listen to porcupines?

A: They have a lot of good points.

Knock, knock.

Who's there?

Dewey.

Dewey who?

Dewey get to play at the beach this summer?

Knock, knock.

Who's there?

Alpaca.

Alpaca who?

Alpaca suitcase for our vacation.

Knock, knock.

Who's there?

Whale.

Whale who?

Whale all you want. I'm not opening the door!

Knock, knock.

Who's there?

Iowa.

Iowa who?

Iowa lot of money, so I can't afford a vacation this year.

Knock, knock.

Who's there?

Jamaica.

Jamaica who?

Please don't Jamaica me tell more knock-knock jokes!

Knock, knock.

Who's there?

Alaska.

Alaska who?

Alaska you to tell me a joke next time!

Q: Why don't sand dollars take a bath?

A: Because they wash up on the shore.

Nick: Do you know the capital of Alaska?

Sam: Yes—don't Juneau?

Sara: What is the capital of Oregon?

Sophia: O.

Knock, knock.

Who's there?

Mushroom.

Mushroom who?

How mushroom do you have left in your suitcase?

Will: Where are there oranges, beaches, and Mickey Mouse?

Bill: In Flori-duh!

Q: What did America say to England when it called after midnight?

A: "Europe?"

Q: What is a sailor's favorite snack?

A: Ships and salsa.

Q: What goes up and down but never moves?

A: A flight of stairs.

Q: How do crabs buy their toys?

A: With sand dollars.

Q: Where does a triceratops like to go swimming?

A: At the dino-shore.

Q: What did the poodle say to the Dalmatian?

A: "I have a bone to pick with you!"

Q: Why wouldn't the jellyfish go down the water slide?

A: Because he was spineless.

Q: Why did the choir go on a cruise?

A: They wanted to hit the high Cs. (seas)

Knock, knock.

Who's there?

Taco.

Taco who?

I could taco 'bout my family vacation all day.

Knock, knock.

Who's there?

Window.

Window who?

Window we finally get there?

Q: What does a trash collector eat for lunch?

A: Junk food.

Knock, knock.

Who's there?

Lettuce.

Lettuce who?

Lettuce go to the beach!

Q: Where is the slipperiest place in the world?

A: Greece.

Mason: Can we have a fish for dinner?

Lucas: Sure, I'll set an extra place at the table.

Knock, knock.

Who's there?

Wheel.

Wheel who?

Wheel be going on our trip soon!

Knock, knock.

Who's there?

Quiche.

Quiche who?

Quiche me before you leave!

Q: Why did the mummy keep hugging her kids good-bye?

A: She thought they were eerie-sistible.

Q: What did the goldfish say after its trip?

A: "What a fin-tastic vacation!"

Q: What kind of money is easy to burn?

A: In-cents.

Knock, knock.

Who's there?

Joe King.

Joe King who?

I'm not Joe King—let me in!

Q: What do spiders eat at a picnic?

A: Corn on the cobweb.

Q: When do birds fly south?

A: In flock-tober.

Q: What happened when the beagle played in the snow?

A: It turned into a chili dog!

Q: How did the famer get rich?

A: He sold his corn stalks. (stocks)

Mason: I ran over a skunk with my bike!

Josh: That stinks.

Q: Why wouldn't the cow get a job?

A: Because he was a meat loafer.

Rob Elliott

HANG-MAN

DOTS!

Each player takes a turn connecting one dot to another dot. The game is played until all the dots become boxes. The player with the most boxes completed at the end is the winner.

Knock, knock.

Who's there?

Gopher.

Gopher who?

I'd gopher a trip abroad if I were you.

Knock, knock.

Who's there?

Pudding.

Pudding who?

I'm pudding away my books for the summer!

Q: Why does coffee get in trouble?

A: Because it's not tea. (naughty)

Knock, knock.

Who's there?

Stopwatch.

Stopwatch who?

Stopwatch you're doing and open the door!

Q: What do you call a crocodile that's always picking fights?

A: An insti-gator.

Q: When is your money stuck in the bank?

A: When you can't budget. (budge it)

Q: What does an archer wear to the ball?

A: A bow tie.

Q: Why did the cow yell at the chicken?

A: It was in a bad moo-d.

Q: Why couldn't the pirate play cards?

A: He was standing on the deck.

Q: Where does a sailor go when he's sick?

A: To the dock.

Q: What is an artist's favorite kind of juice?

A: Crayon-berry.

Knock, knock.

Who's there?

Sweet tea.

Sweet tea who?

Could you be a sweet tea and open the door?

Q: What do you call a reindeer that swims in the ocean?

A: Ru-dolphin.

Q: How does an astronaut pay for his coffee?

A: With Star-bucks!

Q: What did the watch say to its grandfather clock?

A: "I want to wind up like you!"

Q: Why did the pilot paint his jet?

A: He thought it was too plane.

Q: How do artists get to work?

A: They go over the drawbridge.

Q: Why do cows believe everything you say?

A: Because they're so gulli-bull.

Knock, knock.

Who's there?

Tibet.

Tibet who?

Early Tibet, early to rise.

Patient: I broke my leg in two places! What should I do?

Doctor: Don't go to those places!

Q: What do chickens like to eat for dessert?

A: Bak, bak, baklava.

Q: Why did the whale buy a violin?

A: So it could join the orca-stra.

Q: What do you get when you cross a dentist and a boat?

A: A tooth ferry!

Jen: Do you want to see the volcanoes in Hawaii?

Jill: I'd lava to!

Q: Why did the wheels fall off the car?

A: They were tired!

Q: Why did the meteorite go to Hollywood?

A: It wanted to be a star.

Q: Why did the horse keep falling down?

A: It wasn't very stable!

Q: What kind of train needs a tissue?

A: An achoo-choo train!

Q: What do you call a hamburger in space?

A: A meat-eor!

Q: Why don't turtles use the drive-through?

A: They don't like fast food.

Mom: Why do we have to stop at every filling station on the highway?

Dad: It isn't polite to pass gas.

Q: **What do you get when it rains in Paris?**

A: French puddles. (poodles)

Q: **How do you hide in the desert?**

A: Wear camel-flage.

Q: **How do you motivate a lazy mountain?**

A: Light a fire under its butte!

Q: **What kind of car does Mickey Mouse drive?**

A: A Minnie-van.

Q: **Where do elephants keep their spare tires?**

A: In their trunks.

Q: What do you call a horse in space?

A: A saddle-lite.

Q: What do cars wear to stay warm?

A: Hoodies.

Q: How do marine biologists feel about the ocean?

A: They're fin-atics!

Q: How did the lettuce win the race?

A: It got a head start!

Q: How do smart students travel to school?

A: On scholar-ships!

Cowboy Hank: Round up the cattle! Round up the cattle! Round up the cattle!

Cowboy Frank: I herd you the first time.

Q: What do taxi drivers eat for dinner?

A: Corned beef and cab-bage.

Q: Why didn't the melons get married?

A: Because they cantaloupe.

Q: Why don't stars carry luggage on vacation?

A: Because they're traveling light.

Emma: How many antelope live in Africa?

Leah: Probably a gazelle-ion!

Q: How do you get an astronaut's baby to sleep?

A: You rocket.

Q: What kind of boat do you hit with a stick on your birthday?

A: A pin-yacht-a.

Q: What do you call a happy cowboy?

A: A Jolly Rancher.

Knock, knock.

Who's there?

Wafer.

Wafer who?

I've been a wafer too long—let me in!

Tic - **TAC** - Toe

CAN YOU FLY
to
YELLOWSTONE NATIONAL PARK?

Q: How does Saturn clean its rings?

A: With a meteor shower!

Q: When do scuba divers sleep underwater?

A: When they're snore-keling.

Q: Why did the mechanic stop pumping gas?

A: It was a tank-less job.

Q: What kind of car does a dog like to drive?

A: A Land Rover.

Q: Why was the astronaut hungry?

A: Because he missed his launch.

Q: What's a tornado's favorite game?

A: Twister!

Q: Why did the lettuce turn around?

A: It was headed in the wrong direction.

Q: What do you call a crazy spaceman?

A: An astro-nut.

Q: What does the queen of England wear on vacation?

A: A tea shirt.

Q: Which cowboy looks like all the others?

A: The Clone Ranger.

Q: What's an astronaut's favorite drink?

A: Gravi-tea.

Q: Where does a bee wait for a ride?

A: At the buzz stop.

Q: Where does a dog leave its car?

A: In the barking lot.

Q: What did George Washington call his false teeth?

A: Presi-dentures.

Q: What happened when the clam went to the gym?

A: He pulled a mussel.

Q: What is something you always leave behind at the beach?

A: Your footprints.

Q: What is a pirate's favorite Christmas carol?

A: "Deck the Halls."

Q: Why did the hamburger go to the gym?

A: He wanted better buns.

Q: How are flowers like the letter *A*?

A: Bees come after them.

Q: Why do dogs have a great attitude?

A: They like to stay paws-itive.

Q: Why did the criminal go to the gym?

A: He wanted abs of steal.

Q: What kind of bugs like sushi?

A: Wasa-bees.

Q: What did the ocean do when the kids left the beach?

A: It waved good-bye.

Annie: What should I wear when I visit Disneyland?

Amy: A Minnie-skirt!

Q: Why do sharks swim in salt water?

A: Pepper water makes them sneeze!

Q: Why do wasps need to go on vacation?

A: Because they're always busy bees.

Q: Why couldn't the astronaut remember anything?

A: He didn't have enough brain space.

Q: Why couldn't the cat go on the field trip?

A: It forgot its purr-mission slip.

Q: Why did the surfer go to the hair salon?

A: She wanted a permanent wave.

Q: What do you get when you cross a strawberry with a propeller?

A: A jelly-copter!

Q: What kind of fruit do you find in a volcano?

A: A lava-cado!

Q: What do you get when you cross a king with a boat?

A: Leadership!

Q: Where does a farmer stay on vacation?

A: At a hoe-tel.

Q: Why did the tugboat and the yacht

get married?

A: They were in a loving relation-ship.

Q: What does it take to work for the railroad?

A: Lots of training.

Q: How do you send a knight on a mission?

A: You give him a re-quest.

Missy: What do you think of the Grand Canyon?

Mandy: It's gorge-ous!

Q: Why did the astronaut leave the party?

A: He needed some space.

Q: Why can't fishermen get along?

A: They're always de-baiting.

Q: What do you get if you give diamonds to an ambassador?

A: Peace and carats. (peas and carrots)

Q: How do you know if someone ran into your car?

A: Look at the evi-dents.

Q: Why do fishermen always tell the truth?

A: They keep it reel.

Q: Why are trains so focused?

A: They need to stay on track.

Q: Why is the post office a friendly place?

A: It has a lot of outgoing mail.

Knock, knock.

Who's there?

Avenue.

Avenue who?

Avenue packed for your trip yet?

Q: Why were the kids wet when they got to school?

A: They'd ridden in a car pool.

Q: Where do astronauts listen to music?

A: On Neptune.

Q: What do you call a storm that is always rushing around?

A: A hurry-cane.

Q: How do astronauts throw a party?

A: They planet.

Q: Why wouldn't the acrobat perform in winter?

A: He only knew how to do summer-saults.

Q: Why was the sailor upset over his report card?

A: His grades were at C level.

Q: What do you get when you cross a crocodile and a GPS?

A: A navi-gator.

Q: What does Santa wear to the beach?

A: His swim-soot.

Q: Where do penguins go to vote?

A: The South Poll.

Q: How do you get to your accountant's office?

A: In an income taxi.

Q: Where do pirates go to the bathroom?

A: On the poop deck.

Q: What happens when your noodles catch a cold?

A: You get macaroni and sneeze!

Q: Why did the beaver cross the road?

A: To get to the otter side.

Q: What happens when a toad is nervous?

A: It gets worry warts!

Q: How do fish get around the busy ocean?

A: They hail a crab.

Knock, knock.

Who's there?

Izzy.

Izzy who?

Izzy doorbell working or should I

keep knocking?

Q: Why did the lumberjack fall asleep?

A: He was board!

HANG-MAN

DOTS!

Each player takes a turn connecting one dot to another dot. The game is played until all the dots become boxes. The player with the most boxes completed at the end is the winner.

Q: How does a chicken build a house?

A: It lays bricks.

Knock, knock.

Who's there?

Russell.

Russell who?

Russell up some grub. I'm hungry!

Knock, knock.

Who's there?

Handsome.

Handsome who?

Handsome keys over and I'll let myself in.

Q: How was the horse able to pay for all its hay?

A: It had a stable income!

Q: Where did the butcher take his wife on

   a date?

A: To the meatball.

Knock, knock.

Who's there?

Fixture.

Fixture who?

Fixture doorbell and I won't have to knock

so much!

Q: What did Darth Vader say to his son?

A: "I wish you'd be a trooper!"

Q: Why was the tightrope walker stressed out?

A: He was having trouble balancing his schedule.

Knock, knock.

Who's there?

Honeydew.

Honeydew who?

Honeydew you know who's knocking at the door?

Q: Why did the kids get in trouble at Disney World?

A: They were trying to be Goofy!

Joe: Jim, does your doctor do house calls?

Jim: Yes, but your house has to be pretty sick before he'll come over.

Q: What superhero do you want on your baseball team?

A: Batman.

Q: Why couldn't the baker get to his bagels?

A: Because they had lox on them!

Q: Where do birds go for a break?

A: On a re-tweet. (retreat)

Q: **What does a pig say on a hot summer day?**

A: "I'm bacon out here!"

Knock, knock.

Who's there?

Belle.

Belle who?

Belle is fixed, so you don't have to knock!

Q: **What do you get when you cross a cow with a roll of tape?**

A: A beef stick.

Q: **How does the sun kiss the moon?**

A: It puckers its ec-lips.

Q: What do you call tiny glasses?

A: Speck-tacles.

Q: What kind of bird do you eat for dessert?

A: A mag-pie.

Q: Why does everyone ask for Mickey Mouse's autograph?

A: Because he's fa-mouse.

Q: What do you call a zombie elephant?

A: Gro-tusk.

Q: Why did the race-car driver pour stew on his motor?

A: He wanted to soup up the engine.

Q: Why do skunks always show off?

A: They want to be the scent-er of attention.

Q: What did the paper say to the pen?

A: "Write on!"

Q: When is a boxer a comedian?

A: When he delivers a punch line!

Knock, knock.

Who's there?

Leaf.

Leah who?

Leaf the key under the mat so I don't have

to knock!

Q: What kind of car does a tiger drive?

A: A Cat-illac.

Q: Why did Frosty move in with his friends?

A: So he wouldn't feel so ice-olated.

Q: Why was the Tin Man sad on Valentine's Day?

A: Because he was heartless.

Q: What do you call a pig in the dirt?

A: A groundhog.

Q: Why did the snail stay home from school?

A: He was feeling a bit sluggish!

Tongue Twisters

Flat atlas

Pack black pants

Sharks floss fast

Scared squirrels scram

Cranky cramped campers

Knock, knock.

Who's there?

House.

House who?

House it going?

Travis: I was going to tell you a rumor

about germs.

Scott: Why don't you?

Travis: I'm afraid it might spread.

Q: What was Noah's job in the Bible?

A: Ark-itect.

Q: What kind of bird do you send on a quest?

A: A knight owl.

Q: What do you get when you throw cabbage in the snow?

A: Cold slaw.

Q: Why did the orange juice have to go to principal's office?

A: It wouldn't concentrate in class!

Q: Why did the cow cross the road?

A: To get to the udder side.

Q: Why don't canaries want to pay for a vacation?

A: Because they're cheep!

Max: What would happen if a snake swam across the Atlantic?

Jax: It would make hiss-tory!

Q: What do you get when a witch loses her magic?

A: A hex-a-gone.

Q: Where do horses live?

A: In neighborhoods.

Q: Why did the banker go to the football game?

A: He wanted his quarterback!

Q: What is a beluga's favorite drink?

A: Mana-tea.

Q: Where can you find a beaver and an astronaut?

A: In otter space!

Knock, knock.

Who's there?

Gladys.

Gladys who?

I'm Gladys time for summer vacation!

Knock, knock.

Who's there?

Pasture.

Pasture who?

Is it pasture bedtime?

Q: Why is it hard to be a firefighter?

A: You get fired every day!

Q: What's a frog's favorite kind of music?

A: Hip-hop!

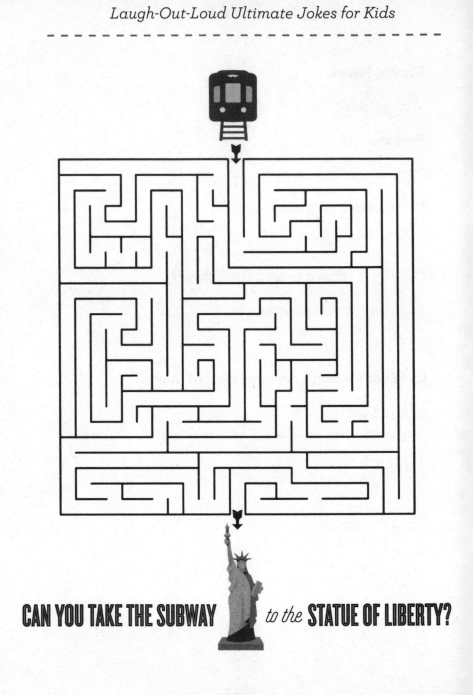

CAN YOU TAKE THE SUBWAY *to the* STATUE OF LIBERTY?

Tic - **TAC** - Toe

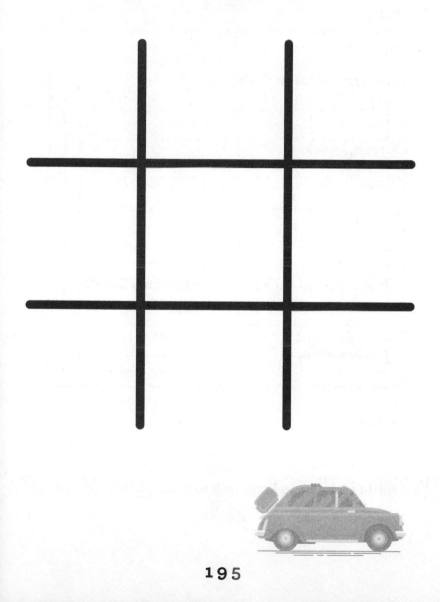

Knock, knock.

Who's there?

Sarah.

Sarah who?

Is Sarah doctor in the house?

Knock, knock.

Who's there?

Russian.

Russian who?

I'm Russian to pack so I don't miss my flight!

Knock, knock.

Who's there?

Anita.

Anita who?

Anita come in so I can talk to you!

Knock, knock.

Who's there?

Iran.

Iran who?

Iran all the way here.

Knock, knock.

Who's there?

Abbott.

Abbott who?

It's Abbott time you answered the door!

Knock, knock.

Who's there?

Yukon.

Yukon who?

Yukon open the door anytime now!

Knock, knock.

Who's there?

Cher.

Cher who?

Cher would be nice if you could join us on vacation!

Knock, knock.

Who's there?

Heaven.

Heaven who?

You heaven a hard time opening the door?

Knock, knock.

Who's there?

Theodore.

Theodore who?

Theodore is jammed and I can't get it open!

Knock, knock.

Who's there?

Hugo.

Hugo who?

When Hugo on vacation I'll miss you!

Q: Why did the chicken quit laying eggs?

A: It was eggs-hausting!

Q: What do they eat in the navy?

A: Submarine sandwiches.

Knock, knock.

Who's there?

Cain.

Cain who?

Cain you tell me some more knock-knock jokes?

George: Have you ever seen a catfish?

Henry: Yes, but I don't think it caught anything.

Q: What kind of lion can you have in the house?

A: A dandelion!

Q: How do you find a train that's lost?

A: Follow its tracks.

Q: Where do you take a fish for an operation?

A: To the sturgeon.

Q: What do you eat for lunch in the desert?

A: Sand-wiches.

Q: Where do Sharpies go on vacation?

A: Pen-sylvania.

Q: What does a cow do on January first?

A: It makes its moo-year's resolution.

Q: What goes tick, tick, woof, woof?

A: A watchdog.

Q: What do you get when you combine a snail and a porcupine?

A: A slowpoke!

Josh: Let me tell you about my underwear.

Jeff: Okay, but please keep it brief. . . .

Q: What do you call a bull that's scared all the time?

A: A cow-ard!

Q: What happens if a kangaroo can't jump?

A: It feels un-hoppy.

Q: When can't you trust a painter?

A: When he's a con artist.

Q: How do you reward the best dentist in town?

A: Give her a plaque!

Q: Why didn't the man trust his bushes?

A: They seemed shady.

Q: When is a car like a frog?

A: When it's being toad!

Q: What do you call a wise dentist?

A: A philo-flosser.

Q: Where do plants like to go to school?

A: The Ivy League.

Q: When is it hard to tell the truth?

A: In Fib-ruary.

Q: What kind of candy do boxers eat?

A: Jawbreakers!

Q: What did the snowman say when he got new glasses?

A: "I-cy!"

Knock, knock.

Who's there?

Saul.

Saul who?

I Saul you were home, so I knocked on the door.

HANG-MAN

DOTS!

Each player takes a turn connecting one dot to another dot. The game is played until all the dots become boxes. The player with the most boxes completed at the end is the winner.

· · · · · · · · · · · · ·

· · · · · · · · · · · · ·

· · · · · · · · · · · · ·

· · · · · · · · · · · · ·

· · · · · · · · · · · · ·

· · · · · · · · · · · · ·

· · · · · · · · · · · · ·

· · · · · · · · · · · · ·

· · · · · · · · · · · · ·

· · · · · · · · · · · · ·

· · · · · · · · · · · · ·

· · · · · · · · · · · · ·

Knock, knock.

Who's there?

Ketchup.

Ketchup who?

Let's ketchup with each other soon.

Knock, knock.

Who's there?

Doris.

Doris who?

The Doris locked or I wouldn't be knocking!

Q: What kind of monkey do you see up in the sky?

A: A hot-air baboon.

Q: **What do dogs have for their birthdays?**

A: Pup-cakes!

Knock, knock.

Who's there?

Johana.

Johana who?

Johana open the door so I can come in?

Q: **Why did the clock get sent to the principal's office?**

A: It wouldn't stop tocking in class!

Q: **Why was the banjo sad?**

A: Everyone was picking on it.

Q: How does a slug cross the ocean?

A: In a snailboat!

Knock, knock.

Who's there?

Utah.

Utah who?

Utah me how to drive—thanks!

Q: What happened when the duck went to the doctor?

A: It got a clean bill of health.

Q: Why is it hard to beat barbers in a race?

A: They take shortcuts!

Knock, knock.

Who's there?

Lena.

Lena who?

Lena little closer and I'll tell you a secret.

Q: Why was the corn feeling sad?

A: It was the laughing-stalk of the farm.

Knock, knock.

Who's there?

Rwanda.

Rwanda who?

Rwanda let me in?

Q: What happens when rabbits fall in love?

A: They live hoppily ever after.

Q: What do you get when you cross a frog and a chair?

A: A toadstool.

Dan: Can you help me find a new dentist?

Sam: You should try mine—he knows the drill!

Knock, knock.

Who's there?

Luke.

Luke who?

Luke outside and you'll see!

Q: How much did the wasp pay for its honey?

A: Nothing, it was a free-bee.

Q: Where does a rabbit go when he needs glasses?

A: A hop-thalmologist.

Q: Where does a peach take a nap?

A: On an apri-cot.

Q: What do boxers eat for dinner?

A: Black-eyed peas.

Q: What kind of dog is always sad?

A: A melan-collie.

Q: What kind of people never get upset?

A: No-mads.

Q: Why did the cow need a tissue?

A: For its moo-cus.

Q: What do you get when you cross a carrot and a pair of scissors?

A: A parsnip.

Q: What kind of bread is the cheapest?

A: Pumper-nickel.

Q: What kind of cheese stays by itself?

A: Prov-alone.

Q: What do you call a cow with a telescope?

A: A star grazer.

Q: What does a crocodile drink at the gym?

A: Gator-ade.

Q: What do clowns eat for lunch?

A: Peanut butter and jolly sandwiches.

Knock, knock.

Who's there?

Elsa.

Elsa who?

Me! Who Elsa do you think it would be?

Q: What do a dog and a watch have in common?

A: They both have ticks.

Q: What did the hen say to its chick?

A: "You're a good egg."

Knock, knock.

Who's there?

Amish.

Amish who?

Amish you and wish you were here!

Q: Why couldn't the spider get anywhere?

A: It was just spinning its wheels.

Q: What do lamps wear to the beach?

A: Shades.

Q: What do TVs wear to the beach?

A: Sun-screen.

Q: What's a bunny's favorite toy?

A: A hula hop.

Q: What's a farmer's favorite movie?

A: *Beauty and the Beets.*

Q: What do you call songs you compose in bed?

A: Sheet music.

Q: Why did the shark cross the road?

A: To get to the other tide.

Knock, knock.

Who's there?

Pencil.

Pencil who?

Your pencil fall down if you don't wear a belt.

Knock, knock.

Who's there?

Wayne.

Wayne who?

Wayne will ruin our day at the beach!

Q: Why did the deer go to the orthodontist?

A: Because it had buck teeth.

Q: What do dogs and sheep have in common?

A: They both have fleece. (fleas)

Q: Who do you call if it's raining cheeseburgers?

A: A meat-eorologist.

CAN YOU DRIVE
to the
GRAND CANYON?

Tic -**TAC** - Toe-

Q: Why was the clock bored?

A: It had too much time on its hands.

Q: Why did the butcher follow the detective?

A: He wanted to go on a steak-out.

Q: What did the dog have to do before going out to play?

A: Ask his paw first.

Q: Why did the pineapple cake turn upside down?

A: It saw the cinnamon roll!

Q: Why couldn't the oyster talk?

A: It clammed up!

Knock, knock.

Who's there?

Butch, Jimmy, and Joe.

Butch, Jimmy, and Joe who?

Butch your arms around me, Jimmy a kiss, and let's Joe to the movies!

Q: What do you do when you're caught outside in a thunderstorm?

A: Hail a cab!

Q: Why was the cook fired from the sandwich shop?

A: He couldn't cut the mustard!

Q: When is a chicken a comedian?

A: When it's at the funny farm!

Q: Why was the boy firing his BB gun in the air?

A: He was shooting the breeze.

Q: Why did the fireman quit his job?

A: He got burned out.

Q: Why did the meteorologist stay in bed?

A: He was feeling under the weather!

- -

Knock, knock.

Who's there?

Ax.

Ax who?

Can I ax you to open the door, please?

Q: What is a shark's favorite game show?

A: *Whale of Fortune.*

Q: Why did the pig get sent to the

principal's office?

A: He was being a ham!

Q: Why did the vampire join the circus?

A: He wanted to be an acro-bat.

Knock, knock.

Who's there?

Toad.

Toad who?

Have I toad you lately that I love you?

Knock, knock.

Who's there?

Panther.

Panther who?

Get me a belt—my panther too loose!

Q: What happened after the boa constrictors got in a fight?

A: They hissed and made up.

Knock, knock.

Who's there?

Chicken.

Chicken who?

I'm chicken under the mat for a key, but I don't see one!

Knock, knock.

Who's there?

Isaac.

Isaac who?

Isaac of these knock-knock jokes!

Q: Why did the monkey need some R & R?

A: He was going bananas!

Knock, knock.

Who's there?

Barry.

Barry who?

It's a Barry good idea for you to let me in.

Q: What is the wealthiest bird?

A: An ost-rich.

Knock, knock.

Who's there?

Hannah.

Hannah who?

Hannah over the keys so I can come in!

Q: Why did the driver cover her eyes?

A: She saw the light was changing.

Knock, knock.

Who's there?

Myth.

Myth who?

I myth you when you're gone!

Knock, knock.

Who's there?

Ari.

Ari who?

Ari there yet?

Q: Who helped the ladybug with her taxes?

A: Her account-ant.

Knock, knock.

Who's there?

Nutella.

Nutella who?

Nutella me when we're going to get there!

Leah: Why do you have ten bowling balls?

Anna: So I'll always have one to spare.

Q: Why did the quarterback carry a paintbrush on the field?

A: So he could touch up his touchdowns.

Q: When do you need medicine on a train?

A: When you have loco-motion sickness.

Q: What did the alien say to the soda?

A: "Take me to your liter."

Q: Why did the librarian need a ladder?

A: So she could reach the tall tales.

Q: What do you call a polar bear that makes coffee?

A: A bear-ista.

Knock, knock.

Who's there?

Juneau.

Juneau who?

Juneau I'm really looking forward to this family vacation!

Knock, knock.

Who's there?

Philip.

Philip who?

Time to Philip the car and hit the road!

Q: What's a horse's favorite snack?

A: Hay-zelnuts.

Q: How did the flea get from one dog to the other?

A: It itch-hiked!

Q: Why can't a giraffe's tongue be twelve inches long?

A: Because then it would be a foot!

Knock, knock.

Who's there?

Abel.

Abel who?

If you're Abel to open the door, I would appreciate it!

Q: How did the hog write a letter?

A: He used his pigpen.

Knock, knock.

Who's there?

Auto.

Auto who?

We auto be there by now!

Q: What did the baby orca do when it got lost?

A: It whaled for its mom!

Knock, knock.

Who's there?

Gideon.

Gideon who?

Gideon the car and let's go!

Q: What is the noisiest animal to own?

A: A trum-pet!

Q: Why shouldn't horses vote?

A: They always say neigh!

Q: Why did the clown need a new red nose?

A: Because his old one smelled funny.

Q: What did the star say to the moon?

A: "I'm falling for you!"

Q: Why did the leopard visit London?

A: He wanted a spot of tea.

Q: Why did the baker keep baking?

A: He was on a roll!

Q: What do you get if your dad gets stuck in the freezer?

A: A Pop-sicle.

Knock, knock.

Who's there?

Italy.

Italy who?

Italy a long time before we stop again, so you better use the restroom!

Q: How do hogs communicate?

A: In pig Latin!

Q: What happened when the baker won the lottery?

A: He shared the dough with his friends!

Q: Why can't you trust a pig with a secret?

A: They're always squealing.

Q: What do you get when you cross an automobile and a dog?

A: A car-pet!

Q: Why was the frog excited to have company?

A: He wanted to show everyone his new pad!

Knock, knock?

Who's there?

Whittle.

Whittle who?

Just a whittle longer and we'll get there!

Q: Why did the banana get fired?

A: Because he split!

Q: How did the teacher know who took the finger paints?

A: They were caught red-handed!

Knock, knock.

Who's there?

Weirdo.

Weirdo who?

Weirdo we go from here?

Q: Why did Dracula need glasses?

A: He was blind as a bat.

Q: Why couldn't the astronauts park the space shuttle on the moon?

A: Because it was full.

Q: Why did Jack Frost drop out of the talent show?

A: He got cold feet!

Q: Why did the science teachers get married?

A: They had great chemistry!

Q: Why did the geometry teacher go to the psychiatrist?

A: He had a lot of problems to solve.

Q: When do chickens go to bed?

A: At ten o'cluck!

Q: When is your mother like a window?

A: When she's being trans-parent.

Q: Why are librarians always late?

A: Because they're overbooked.

Q: Why should you keep a whale happy?

A: If he's sad, he'll start blubbering.

Q: Why did the basketball player smash the stopwatch?

A: His coach said he had to beat the clock to win.

Q: Why did the criminal duck?

A: The judge said he was going to throw the book at him!

Knock, knock.

Who's there?

Howie.

Howie who?

Howie going to get all this stuff in the trunk?

Q: Why was the girl jump-roping down the hall?

A: She was skipping class.

Q: Why did the boy put on boxing gloves before he did his homework?

A: His mom had told him to hit the books.

Q: When does a gorilla put on a suit?

A: When it's got monkey business!

Q: What is a hippo's favorite vegetable?

A: Zoo-cchini.

Q: What vegetable do they serve in prison?

A: Cell-ery.

Q: Why did the deer get a job?

A: It wanted to make a quick buck.

Q: What happened when the witch lost control of her broom?

A: She flew off the handle.

Knock, knock.

Who's there?

Wanda.

Wanda who?

Wanda go to a movie?

Q: Why did the otter do extra homework every night?

A: He was an eager beaver!

Q: Why did the grape jelly and strawberry jelly get together?

A: So they could have a jam session.

Q: Why did the man go to the grocery store after work?

A: His wife told him to bring home the bacon.

Q: Why did the trombone player borrow his friend's trumpet?

A: His teacher said it's rude to toot your own horn!

Q: Why was the weatherman so upset?

A: Somebody stole his thunder.

Q: Why did the cowboy buy a new pair of boots?

A: It was a spur-of-the-moment decision.

Tick - **TAC** - Toe

CAN YOU SAIL
to the
GOLDEN GATE BRIDGE?

Knock, knock.

Who's there?

Gnome.

Gnome who?

There's no place like gnome.

Q: Why will a squirrel always keep a secret?

A: It's a tough nut to crack!

Q: Why were the pigs on the highway?

A: They were road hogs!

Q: Why did the farmer take a hammer to the barn at night?

A: His wife said he should hit the hay!

Q: Why did the vampire join the army?

A: He wanted to go into com-bat.

Q: Why do potatoes make good spies?

A: Their eyes are always peeled!

Q: Why did the boy call the fire department?

A: His money was burning a hole in his pocket!

Knock, knock.

Who's there?

Jell-O.

Jell-O who?

Jell-O, is anybody home?

Knock, knock.

Who's there?

Diesel.

Diesel who?

Diesel be the best trip ever!

Q: Why didn't the corn take a plane?

A: Its ears would pop!

Q: What do you do if your walls are cold?

A: Put on another coat of paint!

Knock, knock.

Who's there?

Audi.

Audi who?

You Audi let me in, it's cold out here!

Q: When is a man like a snake?

A: When he has a frog in his throat.

Q: How do you introduce yourself to a tree?

A: You shake like a leaf.

Tim: I forgot where I put my boomerang.

Scott: Don't worry, it'll come back to you!

Knock, knock.

Who's there?

Weaver.

Weaver who?

Weaver door unlocked next time!

Knock, knock.

Who's there?

Poor me.

Poor me who?

Poor me a cup of water. I'm thirsty!

Q: Why didn't King Arthur go to work?

A: He took the knight off.

Q: What does a queen wear in a thunderstorm?

A: A reign-coat!

Q: Why did the captain quit her job?

A: Because her ship came in.

Q: Where do taxi drivers live?

A: In cab-ins.

Q: Why don't snakes know how much they weigh?

A: They're always losing their scales.

Knock, knock.

Who's there?

Guinevere.

Guinevere who?

Guinevere off the road, I get lost!

Knock, knock.

Who's there?

Roach.

Roach who?

I roach you a postcard from my vacation.

Don't miss these books by
ROB
ELLIOTT!

Keep the laughs coming all year long!

HARPER
An Imprint of HarperCollinsPublishers

www.harpercollinschildrens.com